summer
cultivating

Prize-winning
Maxima
Hybrid pumpkin

Sugar or Pie
Pumpkins
Rich in vitamins A, B-1, B-2,
and niacin–
calcium and iron, too

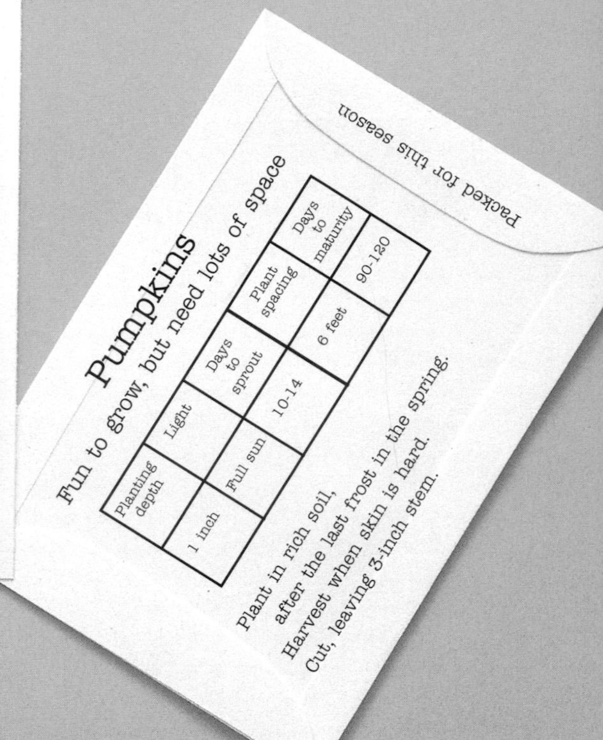
Packed for this season
Pumpkins
Fun to grow, but need lots of space
Planting depth
Light
Days to sprout
Plant spacing
Days to maturity
1 inch
Full sun
10-14
6 feet
90-120
Plant in rich soil,
after the last frost in the spring.
Harvest when skin is hard.
Cut, leaving 3-inch stem.

Heirloom
Pumpkins
Seeds from
original varieties

Excellent for Halloween
Pumpkins
Ideal multi-use pumpkins

Miniature
Pumpkins
Net Wt. 4 g

Written and illustrated by

Nancy Elizabeth Wallace

Marshall Cavendish
New York

Thanks to the Connecticut Agriculture Experiment Station for acting as an invaluable resource.

Marshall Cavendish, 99 White Plains Road, Tarrytown, NY 10591

Library of Congress Cataloging-in-Publication Data
Wallace, Nancy Elizabeth.
Pumpkin Day! / by Nancy Elizabeth Wallace.
p. cm.
Summary: A bunny family picks pumpkins at a local farm and learns
pumpkin facts in the process.
ISBN 0-7614-5128-5
[1. Pumpkin—Fiction. 2. Rabbits—Fiction.] I. Title.
PZ7.W15875 Pu 2002 [E]—dc21 2002000834

The text of this book is set in Geometric 706.
The illustrations are rendered using origami and found paper, scissors and a glue stick.
Book design by Virginia Pope
Printed in Malaysia
First edition
2 4 6 5 3

FOR

the Barr-Russells,
the Feinbergs,
the Gagliardis,
the Grahams,
the Montesi-Levesques,
the Vavra-Lodges,
the Volent-Van Deusens,
sweet families, sweet friends,
and always, for Peter

With love,
N. E. W.

"Daddy, it's Pumpkin Day!" said Trudy one October morning.

"The day we have pumpkin pancakes for breakfast?" he asked.

"Yes!" said Trudy.

"The day we go to pick out pumpkins and buy pumpkin pie?"

"Yes, Daddy!" shouted Trudy and Jack together.

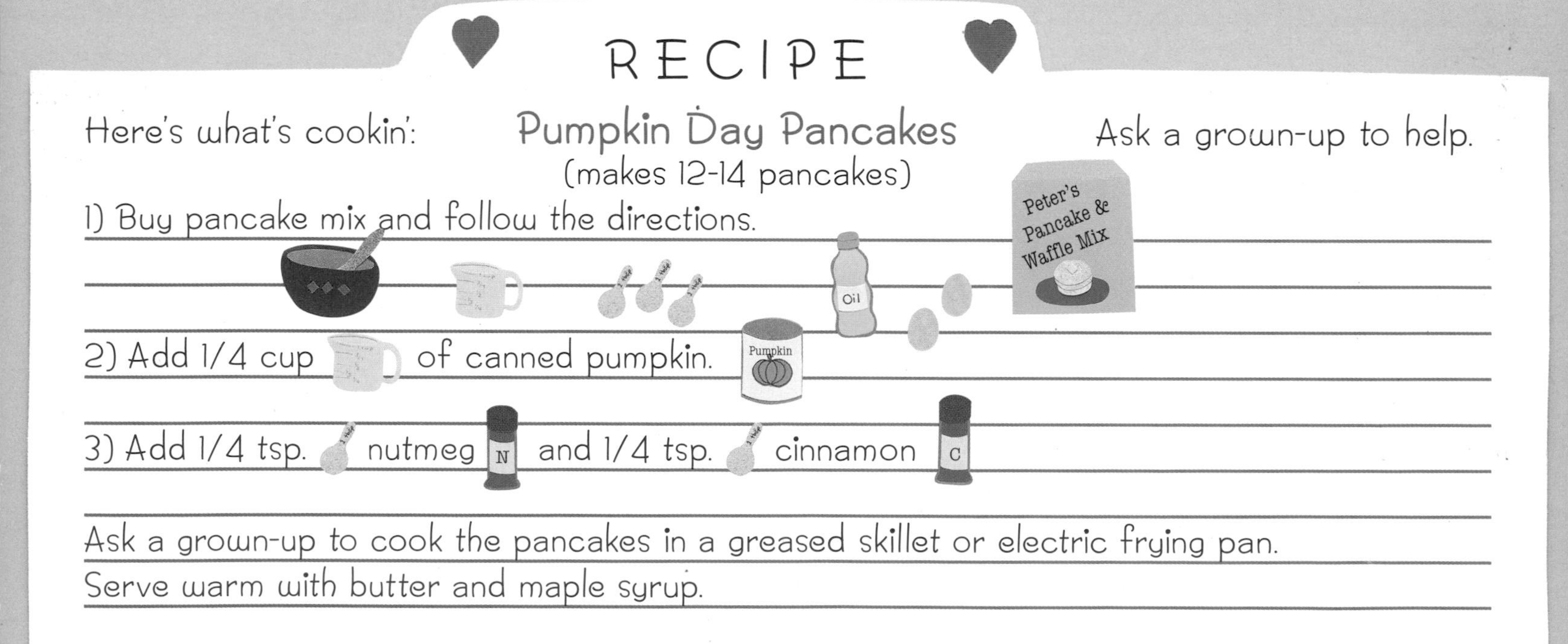

"Well, hooray for Pumpkin Day!" declared Dad. "And pass the pumpkin pancakes, please."

After breakfast, they walked to Pumpkin Hollow Farm. The yellow and orange leaves glowed against the clear blue sky. The fallen leaves made a crunch, crunch, crunch sound under their feet.

Pumpkin Hollow Farm

"Good morning," said Mrs. Bell. "There are lots of pumpkins in the pumpkin patch. We have miniatures, pumpkins for cooking and eating, pumpkins for carving, and one that is very special. I'm sure you'll find it."

"Trudy, what do the signs say?" asked Jack.
Trudy read:

In the fields behind the farm stand, there were small pumpkins and tall pumpkins, round pumpkins and skinny pumpkins, big pumpkins and bumpy pumpkins.

"I like this wrinkly one," said Trudy.

Jack patted the pumpkins. They made a thump sound.

"I want this one!" he said. "Trudy, do pumpkins grow on trees?"

"No Jack. They grow on vines," she answered.

"That's right," said Mrs. Bell. "We plant the seeds in the spring, after the last frost. They sprout, then grow into vines. The vines grow really long, as long as a house, with lots of big leaves."

"At this time of year, the vines are shriveling up. But look. Here's a female pumpkin flower. A pumpkin grows from the swelling at the base of the flower."

"It's green and small," said Trudy. "How do pumpkins grow so big?"

"And orange," added Jack.

Mrs. Bell took some pictures from her pocket.

"Well, with the leaves making food,

and the roots growing in good rich soil,

and with the right amount of sun,

and water,

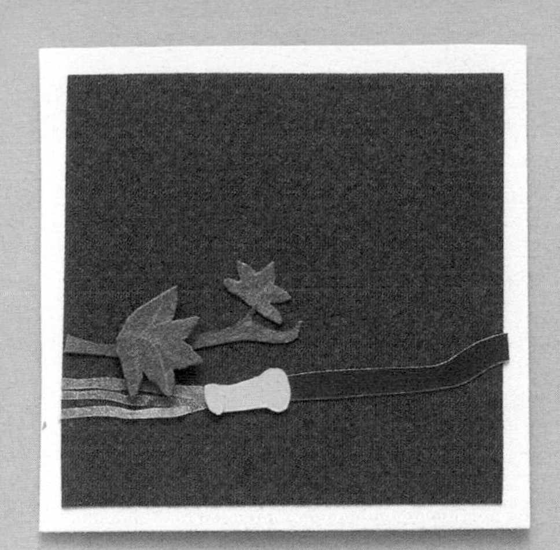

and fertilizer,

and weeding,

and bug control,

the pumpkins will grow from late summer to harvest time.

Night and day they grow bigger."

"And bigger and bigger!"
Trudy and Jack joined in.

"The word pumpkin comes from a Latin word, "pepo."

"Peep-o!" They both giggled.

Mrs. Bell laughed too. "Yes, pepo; it means 'ripened by the sun.' As the pumpkin ripens, what happens to the color?"

"It changes!" exclaimed Trudy.

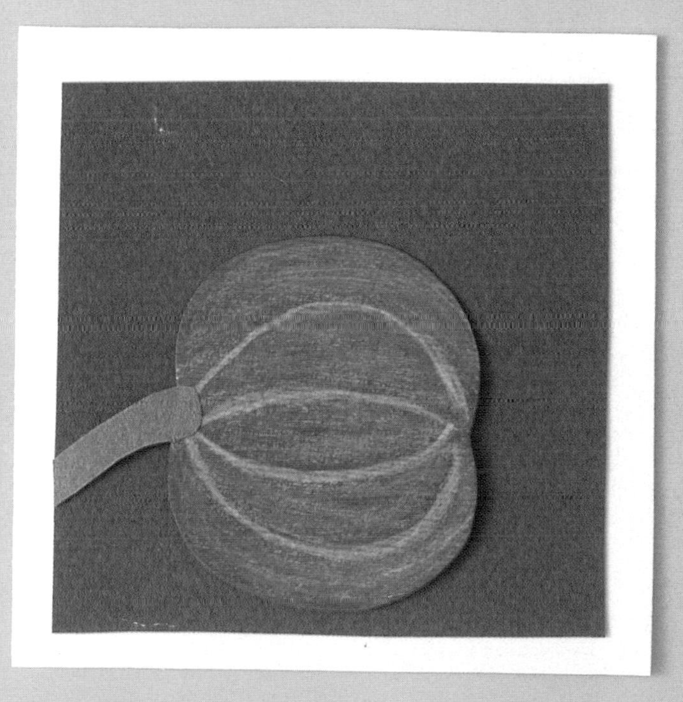

"Look, Trudy, this is the one I want!" yelled Jack.

"Wow!" Trudy shouted.

"It is a Maxima variety," said Mrs. Bell. "Maximas can gain as much as five pounds a day!"

"I wish it were the kind for making pies. It would sure make a lot of them!" said Dad. "Yum."

"Who's going to carry this giant pumpkin home?" Mom asked.

Maximas are the largest fruit in the plant kingdom.

Joke!
What is a pumpkin's favorite sport?

squash!

Then she said, "I will. Can you guess how?

"As a memory. Say 'pumpkin pie,' please."

They picked out their pumpkins and followed Mrs. Bell back to the farm stand.

"What do the signs say, Trudy?" asked Jack.

Trudy read:

"Mom! Look at the baby pumpkins!" said Trudy.

"Those are Baby Boos," said Mom. "They are full grown, just a miniature variety. We can buy a few for decorating. And some pumpkin bread mix and a pumpkin treat for supper."

As soon as they got home, Trudy and Jack practiced drawing pumpkin faces on paper.

Then they drew faces on their pumpkins.

"I want my pumpkin to have ears," said Trudy. "And to be really scary."

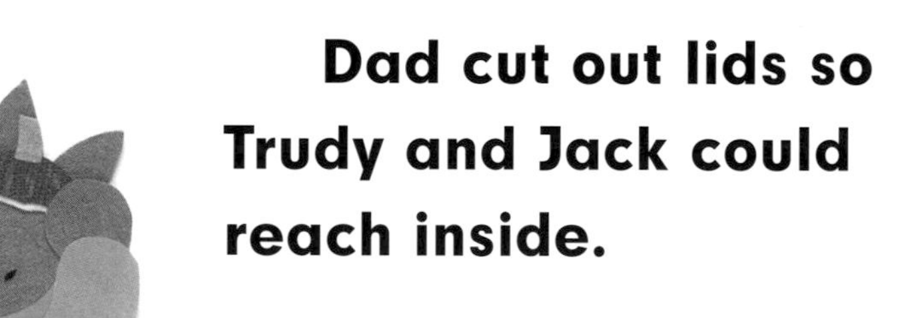

Dad cut out lids so Trudy and Jack could reach inside.

They rolled up their sleeves and scooped.

"It's all stringy and gooey!" said Trudy.

"Look, Trudy, seeds!"

"We can dry some and save them in a jar and plant them next spring," she said.

They scraped the insides clean with big spoons.

Trudy used an apple corer to carve out a nose.

Mom and Dad carved the pumpkins' faces.

"Jack! Our pumpkins are turning into jack-o'-lanterns!" said Trudy.

"In olden times, they hollowed out potatoes and turnips and beets for lanterns. They cut out a little window and put a burning coal inside for light. They called those early jack-o'-lanterns 'bogies,'" said Dad.

"Bogies!" They all giggled.

Mom and Dad and Trudy and Jack made a special Pumpkin Day supper.

RECIPE

Here's what's cookin': **Toasted Jack-O'-Lantern Seeds** Ask a grown-up to help.

1) Preheat the oven to 350°F.

2) Pick out the seeds from the pulp.

3) Pat the seeds dry with a paper towel.

4) Spread the seeds on a cookie sheet.

5) Sprinkle with cooking oil and salt.

6) Ask a grown-up to put the cookie sheet in the oven and to stir the seeds occasionally.

When the seeds are lightly toasted (about 30 minutes), the grown-up should take the cookie sheet out of the oven.

7) Let cool and eat as a snack or sprinkled on salad.

RECIPE

Here's what's cookin': **Trudy's Perfect Pumpkin Muffins** Ask a grown-up to help.
(makes 1 dozen muffins)

1) Buy pumpkin bread mix and follow the directions.

2) Add 1/4 cup of canned pumpkin. Stir until blended.

3) Pour the batter into greased and floured muffin tins.

4) Ask a grown-up to put the muffin tins in the oven and to take them out. They will be done when a toothpick comes out clean (about 20-25 minutes).

5) Serve warm or cool. Tasty with cream cheese.

They ate pumpkin muffins, toasted pumpkin seeds sprinkled on salad, and for dessert, pumpkin pie!

Trudy looked over at the pumpkins.
Finally it was dark outside.
"Mom," she whispered. "It's time!"
Jack turned out the lights.

oooOOOOOOOOO!

BOO!

Fall
harvesting